Just in Rhyme

FAMILY FAVOURITES

by Toni McKay-Lawton

Illustrated by Eddie Manning

Ransom

tortoises are very slow
some people call them ploddy
i think it must be their short
                          legs
or perhaps it's their stout body

pussycats are fat and fluffy
with whiskers on their faces
they like to go outside and
sleep
curled up in their favourite
places

a dog is quite a playful chap
who really likes to bark
but best of all he loves to walk
and chase balls in the park

a mouse it is a little thing
that scuttles round at night
it's only hunting for a snack
so don't you dare take fright

a rat can be a friend to you
he really is very sweet
but perhaps you shouldn't say
hello
if you meet him on the street